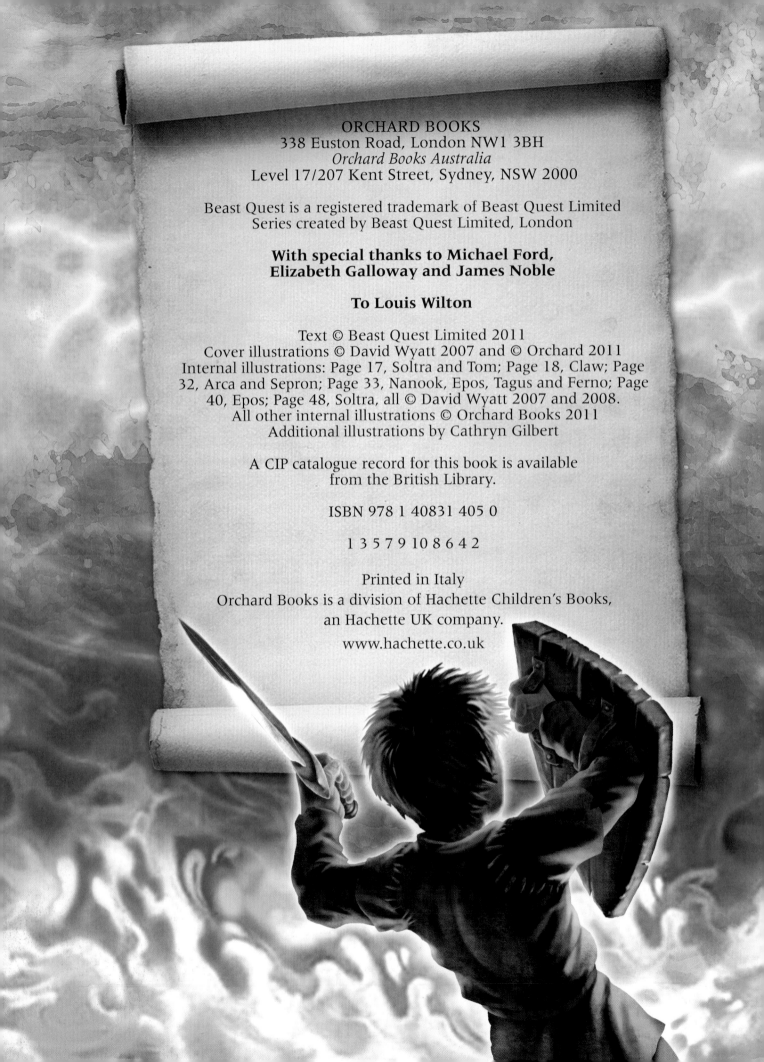

ORCHARD BOOKS
338 Euston Road, London NW1 3BH
Orchard Books Australia
Level 17/207 Kent Street, Sydney, NSW 2000

Beast Quest is a registered trademark of Beast Quest Limited
Series created by Beast Quest Limited, London

**With special thanks to Michael Ford,
Elizabeth Galloway and James Noble**

To Louis Wilton

A CIP catalogue record for this book is available
from the British Library.

ISBN 978 1 40831 405 0

1 3 5 7 9 10 8 6 4 2

Printed in Italy
Orchard Books is a division of Hachette Children's Books,
an Hachette UK company.

www.hachette.co.uk

ANNUAL 2012

This book belongs to

.........James miller.........

CONTENTS

8–11   The Story So Far

12–13   Make Tom's Shield

14–15   Heroes and Villains: Chapter 1

16   Who am I?

17   Cross the Deadly Marshes

18–19   Claw vs Rashouk

20   Sanpao the Pirate King

21   Walk the Plank

22–23   Draw Your Own Beast Quest

24   An Introduction to Wizards

25   Petra's Wicked Wizard Quiz

26–27   Heroes and Villains: Chapter 2

28–29   Dive into the Black Ocean!

30–31   Elenna

32–33   The Good Beasts of Avantia

34–35   Design Your Own Kragos and Kildor

36–37   Vespick vs Kaymon

38–39   Heroes and Villains: Chapter 3

40   Tom's Quest Memories

41   What Can You See?

42   Test Your Memory

43   Petra's Spell

44–45   The Warrior's Sword

46   Petra's Potion

47   Petra's Puzzle

48–49   Spaghetti and Eyeballs

50–51   Heroes and Villains: Chapter 4

52–53   Arax vs Koldo

54   Trapped!

55   Who is the Real Aduro?

56–57   Beast Attack!

58   Showdown with Sanpao!

59   While There's Blood In Your Veins...

60–61   Answers

CAN YOU STOP SANPAO?

Sanpao the Pirate King is sailing through the pages of this annual! As you read, look out for six pictures of his ship. Each has a riddle for you to solve. Keep your answers in a safe place – you will need them to do battle later with the evil Pirate King...

Welcome,
followers of the Quest!

A new threat has arrived in Avantia – a villain with the magical cunning of Malvel, combined with a warrior's fighting skill.

His name is Sanpao, the Pirate King.

Avantia needs you to drive off its latest enemy. Throughout this annual, you will be set fiendishly difficult quizzes and activities. Each time you succeed, Sanpao's hold over Avantia grows weaker.

Beast's eye

Claw

Trident

Hidden among the pages of this book are six magical tokens that will help you in your final battle against the Pirate King. Can you find them?

Fang

Scale

Throwing star

Keep your eyes open and your heart strong. Good luck, my friend…

Tom

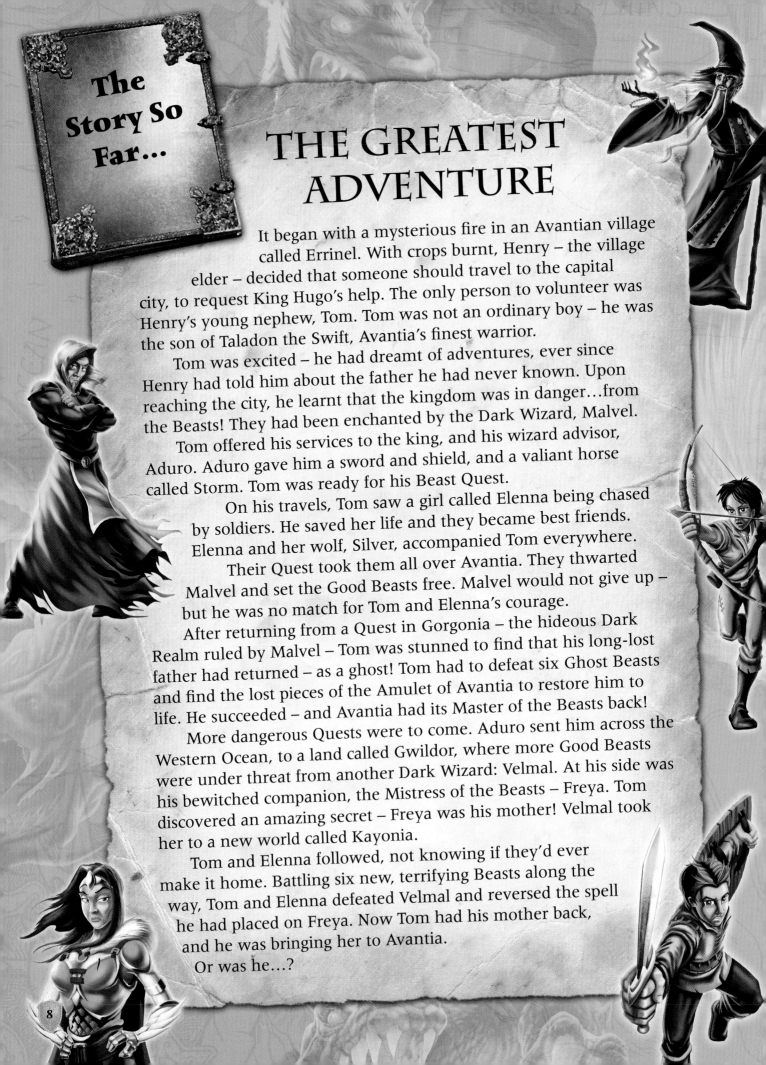

THE GREATEST ADVENTURE

It began with a mysterious fire in an Avantian village called Errinel. With crops burnt, Henry – the village elder – decided that someone should travel to the capital city, to request King Hugo's help. The only person to volunteer was Henry's young nephew, Tom. Tom was not an ordinary boy – he was the son of Taladon the Swift, Avantia's finest warrior.

Tom was excited – he had dreamt of adventures, ever since Henry had told him about the father he had never known. Upon reaching the city, he learnt that the kingdom was in danger…from the Beasts! They had been enchanted by the Dark Wizard, Malvel.

Tom offered his services to the king, and his wizard advisor, Aduro. Aduro gave him a sword and shield, and a valiant horse called Storm. Tom was ready for his Beast Quest.

On his travels, Tom saw a girl called Elenna being chased by soldiers. He saved her life and they became best friends. Elenna and her wolf, Silver, accompanied Tom everywhere.

Their Quest took them all over Avantia. They thwarted Malvel and set the Good Beasts free. Malvel would not give up – but he was no match for Tom and Elenna's courage.

After returning from a Quest in Gorgonia – the hideous Dark Realm ruled by Malvel – Tom was stunned to find that his long-lost father had returned – as a ghost! Tom had to defeat six Ghost Beasts and find the lost pieces of the Amulet of Avantia to restore him to life. He succeeded – and Avantia had its Master of the Beasts back!

More dangerous Quests were to come. Aduro sent him across the Western Ocean, to a land called Gwildor, where more Good Beasts were under threat from another Dark Wizard: Velmal. At his side was his bewitched companion, the Mistress of the Beasts – Freya. Tom discovered an amazing secret – Freya was his mother! Velmal took her to a new world called Kayonia.

Tom and Elenna followed, not knowing if they'd ever make it home. Battling six new, terrifying Beasts along the way, Tom and Elenna defeated Velmal and reversed the spell he had placed on Freya. Now Tom had his mother back, and he was bringing her to Avantia.

Or was he…?

THE LOST WORLD

On their next adventure, Tom, Elenna and Freya – Tom's mother – stepped through a portal into what they thought was the Kingdom of Avantia. Things looked the same, but with one crucial difference – a black flag was flying over the King's Palace. When they went inside they discovered Malvel on King Hugo's throne. He used his evil magic to kill their friend Marc, Aduro's young apprentice. Then he ordered his soldiers to throw them in jail.

After escaping, Tom and his companions discovered that they were not in Avantia at all, but a strange parallel version of their home kingdom – Tavania. This new kingdom was under threat from Malvel's magic. Its glass-domed sky had ripped open at six points across the kingdom, displacing its Good Beasts from their natural habitats, and making them angry and destructive.

Tom had to use all his wits to confront the Beasts and send them home. Once he had achieved that, he led a rebellion against Malvel. With the help of the kingdom's wizard, Oradu, they opened a portal back to Avantia, and dragged Malvel through.

Unfortunately, not all of Tom's companions made it home with him…

ELLIK THE LIGHTNING HORROR

One of the toughest Beasts Tom faced in Tavania was Ellik, who had a massive, snake-like body and a long, deadly tongue. As if that wasn't enough, Tom also had to avoid her bolts of lightning!

TOM'S WEAPONS

Tom can't survive his Beast Quests through bravery alone. Along the way, he has picked up valuable tokens that help him out of tough scrapes. His shield contains special gifts given to him by the Good Beasts, and the jewels in his belt give him some brilliant powers – like being able to send his own shadow ahead to look for danger!

THE PIRATE KING

Tom and Elenna might have defeated Malvel, but Freya and Silver were trapped in Tavania. Meanwhile, Aduro had sent Taladon on a search for the magical Tree of Being. The wizard believed that the Tree held the key to bringing their friends back to Avantia. But Taladon was not the only one searching for the Tree…

When his father returned, battered and bloodied, to the palace, Tom knew that Taladon had encountered perhaps the deadliest foe he had yet faced. And so it proved with the arrival of the Pirate King, Sanpao.

Commanding a ship that could fly as well as float, Sanpao and his vicious pirate crew rampaged across the kingdom, hunting the Tree of Being so that they could steal its magical power. Tom and Elenna entered a desperate race to reach the Tree first.

Standing in their way were six terrifying Beasts. Tom and Elenna fought bravely, until the final battle in the courtyard of King Hugo's Palace, where the Tree of Being had sprouted. Avantia's greatest young heroes joined the king's army in defending the precious Tree, allowing Freya and Silver to make it home at last through the portal!

HECTON THE BODY-SNATCHER

This terrifying Beast stalked the Vanished Woodland, a secret forest in the east. His hideous cloak contained the souls and bodies of the victims he consumed. Tom had to use all of his wits to avoid the Beast's deadly net and trident, and all of his strength to set Hecton's victims free.

THE TREE OF BEING

The mysterious Tree of Being always springs from the ground where you least expect it, and its magic has been used for both good and evil. While Tom used it to open the portal that would bring home Freya and Silver, Sanpao stole a branch for use on his ship's mast – giving the ship the ability to fly.

THE WARLOCK'S STAFF

Avantia's heroes may have thwarted the Pirate King, but their heroic actions had a terrible consequence – Malvel used the courtyard battle as a distraction in his escape from the dungeon!

Now, he and his apprentice, Petra, are on their most deadly mission yet. They have stolen the most powerful magical artefact in all the known worlds – the Warlock's Staff!

Made of wood from the Tree of Being, the Warlock's Staff can be used for good – but in the wrong hands, it can be twisted to evil. Malvel has taken the staff to the distant, mysterious realm called Seraph, where he plans to burn it in the Eternal Flame. If he succeeds, he will become the most powerful Wizard in all the known kingdoms, and not even the combined force of Tom, Elenna, Taladon and Aduro will be able to stop him.

A new kingdom, the most deadly Quest yet… Will Tom and Elenna survive?

A HERO'S PARENTS

Tom loves his life of Beast Quests, but it comes at a price – each new challenge takes him away from his parents. Tom is happy to have his family reunited, even though he knows it cannot last. Soon, the time will come when his mother must return to Gwildor and continue her duties as Mistress of the Beasts.

SILVER THE WILD TERROR

In the land of Seraph, Malvel and Petra created Beasts by poisoning animals and people, turning them into creatures of destruction.

This time, the evil wizard has gone too far – he's turned Silver into a ferocious Wolf-Beast!

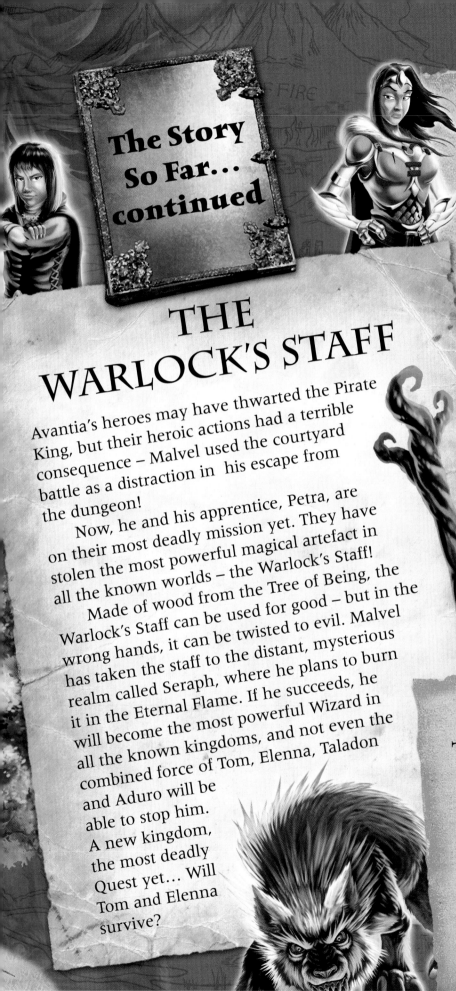

MAKE TOM'S SHIELD

Everybody needs protection in battle – even the bravest boy in Avantia! Tom's faithful shield is decorated with six magical tokens, giving him extra powers on his Beast Quests.

Now you can make your own enchanted shield, designed to fit your size! Craft it with care and keep it close – a warrior never knows when danger will loom near.

YOU WILL NEED:

A TAPE MEASURE

PENCIL

PAPER

LARGE CARDBOARD BOX

RULER

SCISSORS OR CRAFT KNIFE

DUCT TAPE

TRACING PAPER

OLD NEWSPAPERS

POSTER PAINT AND FELT-TIPPED PENS

PAINTBRUSH

PAPER GLUE

1 Ask a trusted companion to measure the length of your arm from the middle of your palm to the inside of your elbow. Write the measurement on a scrap of paper.

2 Flatten out a large cardboard box. On the inside, draw out a shield shape that is 20cm wider than the length of your arm. When you've sketched the basic shape, use a ruler to neaten up the edges.

3 Ask an adult to help you cut the shield out using scissors or a craft knife.

4 When the shield is cut out, lay it back on the empty cardboard box and trace the shape one more time. Cut this shield out too.

5 Hold one of the shields up against your arm, then ask your helper to mark a vertical line where your palm and elbow touch the cardboard.

6 Ask an adult to score two horizontal slits above and below each of these lines, about an arm width apart.

7 Cut off a strip of duct tape around 30cm long. Carefully turn the strip so that the sticky side is facing outwards, then thread it through the first set of slits on the shields. When the loop of tape is wide enough for your arm to slide through, fix the sticky side down on the back. Do this again to create the second arm strap.

8 Wind duct tape round both arms straps, so that all the sticky areas are covered. Smooth it over carefully so the shield will be easy to hold. Set the shield to one side.

9 Copy the six magical tokens onto a piece of tracing paper, adjusting the size so they will fit on the front of your shield. Now take your second cardboard shield and transfer the shapes on top.

10 Ask an adult to very carefully cut out the six shapes using a craft knife, taking care not to cut through to the edge of the shield.

11 Place your second shield and the tokens on a sheet of newspaper, then paint them to match Tom's.

Use felt-tipped pens to pick out the grain of the wood and the iron rivets that hold your shield together!

12 When the paint has dried, cover the front of the first shield with a layer of paper glue. Now carefully press the back of the painted shield onto this. When the glue has set, your shield will be ready! Carefully push the six tokens into their slots, ready for whenever you need them!

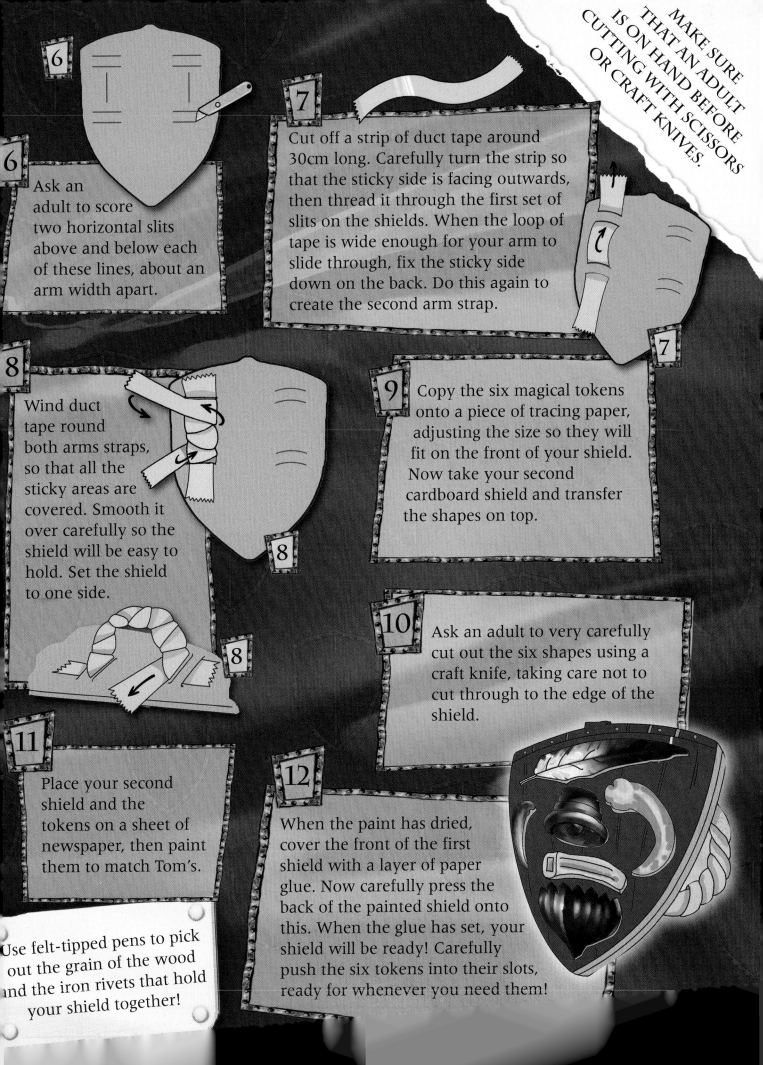

HEROES AND VILLAINS

Greetings, readers. It isn't often I, Malvel the Dark Wizard, have the chance to tell my side of the story. I wasn't always an outcast. Once upon a time, I was just a young wizard, apprenticed to Aduro...

King Theo of Avantia was hosting a jousting tournament in the palace grounds. All the nobles of the land had gathered to witness the spectacle. I stood at the back, watching everything.

The crowd fell silent as the two mounted challengers lined up opposite each other. It looked an uneven match – at one end, upright on a grey stallion, sat the King's son, Prince Hugo. His armour shone like gold, and he held his lance as though it weighed nothing. Facing him, on a horse borrowed from the stables, sat a boy from the village of Errinel, called Taladon. Barely thirteen years old, he wore battered armour. The plates were rusted and dented, the helmet was too big, but he gripped his lance confidently as he waved to the crowd.

I never liked him, even then.

As the bugle sounded, they spurred their steeds and galloped forwards. The crowd held its breath until...*SMASH!*

Prince Hugo's lance shattered on Taladon's shield. At the same time, the boy's lance lifted the Prince from the saddle, throwing him to the ground. The crowd roared.

A lucky strike! I thought. Hugo should be ashamed of himself for being beaten by a peasant!

Taladon reined in his horse and leapt down. He rushed to the fallen Prince's side and offered his hand.

"Are you all right?" I heard him ask.

Prince Hugo, sitting up, lifted his helmet's face-guard. He took the boy's hand and got to his feet. "The day is yours, young Taladon!" he laughed.

The crowd cheered to see that the two opponents were still friends. With a flick of his staff, Aduro mended the Prince's shattered lance. The idiot nobles *oohed* and *aahed*. My hands balled into fists. Magic was for destruction, not tricks. *I'd show them all, one day!*

As a small group of people lifted Taladon onto their shoulders, I saw a soldier approach and ascend the steps to King Theo's platform. The soldier leant down to the King's ear and whispered something. Even from a distance, I saw the blood drain from the old King's face as he turned to speak to Aduro. My master nodded back. Together they entered the palace with the soldier.

Something's afoot! I thought. *And I won't be kept in the dark.*

I followed them into the cool dark corridors, padding quietly a few steps behind. Soon I reached the King's private chamber. The soldier guarding the doorway thrust his pike across, barring my entry.

"King Theo said he's not to be disturbed, Master Malvel," he said.

Foolish wretch! I wanted to use a spell on him then, to turn his bones to jelly, but I restrained my urge. "Of course," I said politely. I retreated a few steps, then uttered a spell: "Never fear thou cannot spy, let me cast my wizard's eye."

An old trick, which allowed me to see through walls. I'd learnt it while snooping through Aduro's books of magic. The stone before me disappeared and I saw into the chamber. A man in tattered rags, his face scarred by a half-healed wound, knelt before the King.

"…the Gorgonians will come through the portal any day now," he said. "Their army will strike at Avantia. I almost didn't make it here to tell you."

"Thank you for this information, Kerlo," said Aduro. He looked to the soldier. "Take this brave man to the infirmary."

Once they had left, the King looked at Aduro gravely. "We must mobilise the Beasts to protect the Kingdom."

Aduro shook his head. "It's too risky. We haven't yet replaced the dead Master of the Beasts. We haven't even recovered his shield from the caves."

So that's where it is! I thought. For months Aduro had refused to tell me where the magical shield had been lost. He'd never trusted me! Well, now I knew, and soon its power would be mine.

Before I could flee, Aduro strode out of the door and saw me.

"What are you doing here?" he asked, surprised.

"Looking for you, Master," I cringed.

"Well, I have an important mission for you," he said.

This is it! I thought. *He's going to ask me to find the shield. I'll be wizard and Master of the Beasts – all at once!*

"Yes, Master?" I said.

"Go and fetch the boy, Taladon," Aduro replied.

To be continued…

WHO AM I?

It's not just a taste for battle and adventure that makes a good Master of the Beasts – you also have to know everything about the magical creatures of Avantia and beyond. Find out if YOU have what it takes by looking at the clues below to name a mystery Beast. The fewer clues you need, the better chance you have of filling Taladon's shoes.

CLUES

DANGER · DESTINY

1 I ONCE TRAVELLED THE KINGDOM WITH A RIDER CALLED TANNER.

2 I AM THE OLDEST OF THE GOOD BEASTS.

3 MY HOME IS THE STONEWIN VOLCANO.

4 I AM AT MY BEST AMONGST FLAMES.

5 MY TALON GIVES TOM HEALING POWERS.

The Beast is:

E P O S

Answers can be found on pages 60-61

Cross the Deadly Marshes

Can you help Tom cross the marsh, from left to right, without being captured by Soltra the Stone Charmer? Look closely at the stepping stones until you find the word that will lead to the other side. But be careful – one mistake spells Tom's doom…

Answers can be found on pages 60-61

Claw vs Rashouk

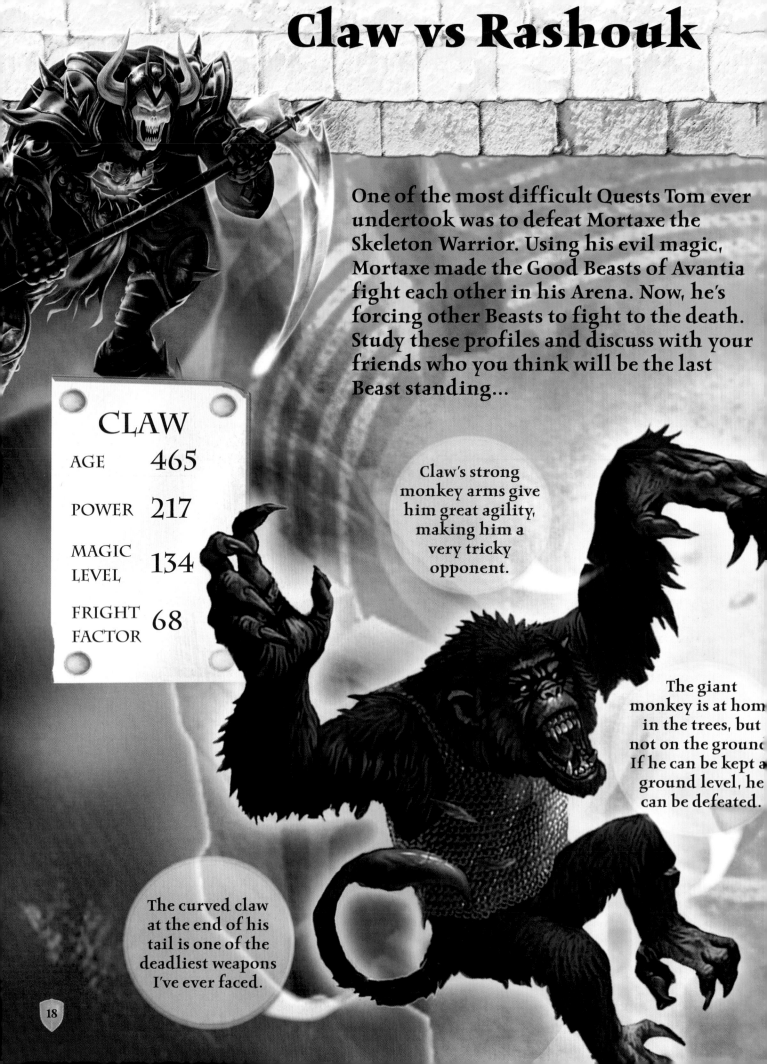

One of the most difficult Quests Tom ever undertook was to defeat Mortaxe the Skeleton Warrior. Using his evil magic, Mortaxe made the Good Beasts of Avantia fight each other in his Arena. Now, he's forcing other Beasts to fight to the death. Study these profiles and discuss with your friends who you think will be the last Beast standing...

CLAW

AGE	465
POWER	217
MAGIC LEVEL	134
FRIGHT FACTOR	68

Claw's strong monkey arms give him great agility, making him a very tricky opponent.

The giant monkey is at hom in the trees, but not on the groun If he can be kept a ground level, he can be defeated.

The curved claw at the end of his tail is one of the deadliest weapons I've ever faced.

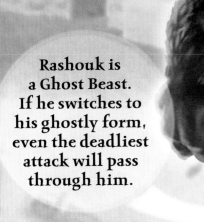

RASHOUK

AGE	321
POWER	165
MAGIC LEVEL	154
FRIGHT FACTOR	81

Rashouk is a Ghost Beast. If he switches to his ghostly form, even the deadliest attack will pass through him.

If Rashouk manages to scratch you with his hideous yellow nails, the fight is over – you will be turned to stone. However, if you can cut these nails off, he can be defeated.

Rashouk may be huge, but his size makes him slow. If an opponent can stop him using his ghostly form, he will be vulnerable to quick attacks.

TOM SAYS:
"Mortaxe's Arena can barely contain these two giant Beasts. When I fought them, I only just managed to escape with my life. Who do YOU think will win this duel?"

AND THE WINNER IS...
Rashouk

SANPAO THE PIRATE KING

SANPAO'S SERVANTS

As well as his cruel pirates, Sanpao has another crew, too: six deadly Beasts!

 Kronus the Clawed Menace

 Koron, Jaws of Death

 Bloodboar the Buried Doom

 Torno the Hurricane Dragon

 Hecton the Body-Snatcher

 Balisk the Water Snake

Sanpao is king of the Pirates of Makai, a cut-throat band of scoundrels. They travel from land to land, looting and terrorizing anyone who stands in their way.

Before Sanpao came to power, the Pirates of Makai were ruled by his brother, Polkai. Sanpao spread lies about Polkai among the pirates, persuading them that Polkai was a coward who wanted to keep all the treasure for himself. Cheered on by the rest of the crew, Sanpao forced Polkai to walk the plank – cackling with delight as his own brother fell into shark-infested waters.

 SHIP AHOY!

The main mast of the pirate ship is made from a branch of the Tree of Being, which gives the vessel its power to fly. The pirates aren't restricted to attacking the coast, they can also attack inland. When villagers and townspeople see the ship's hull bearing down on them, they flee. Sanpao and his men then loot their homes. The ship's sails are blood-red and decorated with the symbol of the Pirates of Makai: a terrifying Beast's skull with horns.

20

WALK THE PLANK

Phew! You're back on board.

You're a prisoner on Sanpao's pirate ship – and he's decided you should walk the plank! Will you make it back to the ship or topple over the brink?

You could play with a friend too. Take it in turns to toss the coin, and see who can move their counter back to the ship first.

HOW TO PLAY

You'll need a coin and a counter. Place your counter on the footprints and toss the coin. If it's TAILS, move TWO SPACES down towards the sea. But if it's HEADS, move ONE SPACE up – towards the ship! Keep playing until you're either safely on the ship or swimming with the sharks.

Oh no! You'll have to take your chances with the sharks…

Draw Your Own Beast Quest

Tom has fought many spectacular battles against terrifying Beasts. Here, you can bring to life one of his greatest Quests – against Bloodboar the Buried Doom. Use a pencil to draw in the blank panels, and tell the story of Tom versus Bloodboar in your own unique style!

1 The courtyard walls were not strong enough to keep out Bloodboar. The Beast had arrived – and only Tom and Elenna could defeat him.

2 From his floating pirate ship, evil Sanpao ordered the Beast to uproot the magical Tree of Being. Tom could not let that happen!

3 Tom and Elenna goaded the Beast into charging them, jumping out of the way at the very last second. This made Bloodboar angry.

4 Tom leapt onto the Beast's back in an effort to control him. Up close, he could see that the Beast's bone armour did not grow from its hide. Maybe he could prise it off?

5 Bloodboar kicked out his hind-legs, and threw Tom off. Our hero was knocked unconscious!

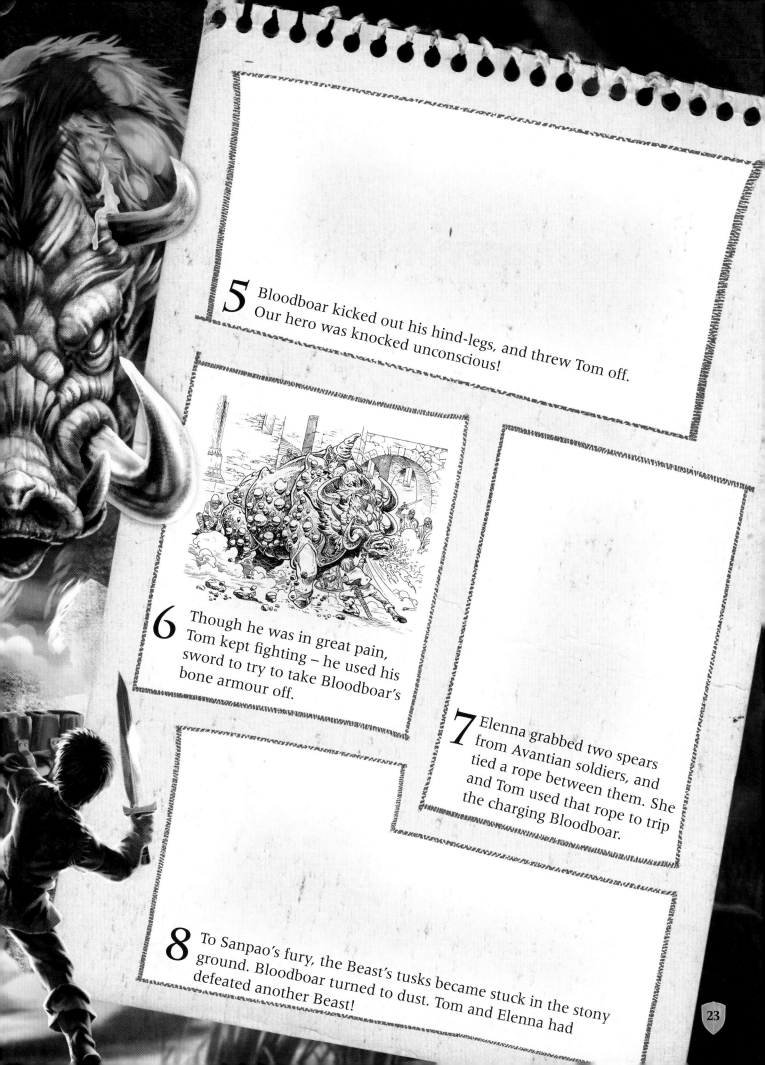

6 Though he was in great pain, Tom kept fighting – he used his sword to try to take Bloodboar's bone armour off.

7 Elenna grabbed two spears from Avantian soldiers, and tied a rope between them. She and Tom used that rope to trip the charging Bloodboar.

8 To Sanpao's fury, the Beast's tusks became stuck in the stony ground. Bloodboar turned to dust. Tom and Elenna had defeated another Beast!

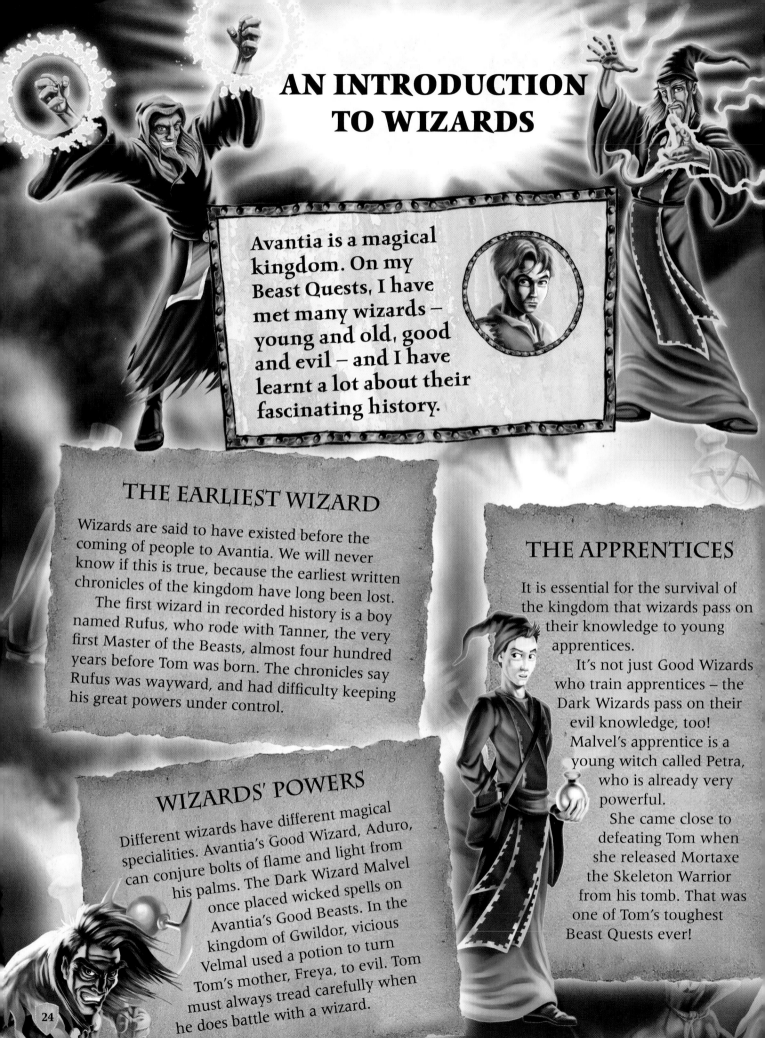

AN INTRODUCTION TO WIZARDS

Avantia is a magical kingdom. On my Beast Quests, I have met many wizards – young and old, good and evil – and I have learnt a lot about their fascinating history.

THE EARLIEST WIZARD

Wizards are said to have existed before the coming of people to Avantia. We will never know if this is true, because the earliest written chronicles of the kingdom have long been lost.

The first wizard in recorded history is a boy named Rufus, who rode with Tanner, the very first Master of the Beasts, almost four hundred years before Tom was born. The chronicles say Rufus was wayward, and had difficulty keeping his great powers under control.

WIZARDS' POWERS

Different wizards have different magical specialities. Avantia's Good Wizard, Aduro, can conjure bolts of flame and light from his palms. The Dark Wizard Malvel once placed wicked spells on Avantia's Good Beasts. In the kingdom of Gwildor, vicious Velmal used a potion to turn Tom's mother, Freya, to evil. Tom must always tread carefully when he does battle with a wizard.

THE APPRENTICES

It is essential for the survival of the kingdom that wizards pass on their knowledge to young apprentices.

It's not just Good Wizards who train apprentices – the Dark Wizards pass on their evil knowledge, too! Malvel's apprentice is a young witch called Petra, who is already very powerful.

She came close to defeating Tom when she released Mortaxe the Skeleton Warrior from his tomb. That was one of Tom's toughest Beast Quests ever!

Petra's Wicked Wizard Quiz

So you've learnt some things about wizards, but how much do you really know? Is your mind as sharp as Tom's sword, or as soft as mud? Tackle my Wizard Quiz below and find out!

2

HOW OLD IS AVANTIA'S GOOD WIZARD, ADURO?

A: 100
B: 70
C: 50

Fish, penguins, tadpoles and seals can all _ _ _ _ _

1

WHO IS THE DARK WIZARD OF GWILDOR?

A: Velmal
B: Jonah
C: Malvel

3

MALVEL HAS A CASTLE IN WHICH REGION OF GORGONIA?

A: The North
B: The East
C: The West

4

WHO KILLED MARC, ADURO'S APPRENTICE?

A: Rufus
B: Malvel
C: Me, Petra

5

WHAT WAS THE NAME OF TAVANIA'S GOOD WIZARD?

A: Dalaton
B: Kerlo
C: Oradu

Answers can be found on pages 60-61

HEROES AND VILLAINS

I, Taladon, was as surprised as anyone to be given a mission at the age of thirteen. But Aduro told me that King Theo was relying on me. So I heeded the call.

I looked back over my shoulder and saw the purple tear in the sky. The portal was growing stronger by the hour, and soon nothing would stop the army of Gorgonians flooding into Avantia.

"Not if I have anything to do with it," I muttered.

I spurred my horse harder, his hooves rattling the rickety planks of the bridge over the Winding River. Prince Hugo had kindly lent me his own stallion. Its coat sparkled silver in the light of dusk.

I'd come to the palace that day thinking I'd get knocked out in the first round of the jousting competition. As it turned out, one after the other my opponents fell. The kindly wizard said he'd seen something special about me. But even then, as I followed the riverbank, I wasn't sure.

"You're the only one who can stop this," Aduro had said.

"While there's blood in my veins, I'll do my best," I replied.

Hands gripping the reins, I leant low over the stallion's back. I'd never been this far south along the Winding River, but I'd heard of the caves. As youngsters we were told not to go near them.

Our parents said a dragon lived inside, and until that day I'd always thought it was a lie to stop us getting into trouble. But today Aduro had told me that the myths were true…

"Inside the cave," he'd said, "you must find the shield."

"Shield?"

He had nodded. "It belonged to a very brave man, before he…before he was killed. With the shield on your arm, you can control the Beast in the cave."

"And without it?" I asked.

"Without it you'll be in grave danger," he had replied.

I had tried not to show my fear in front of the King and the wizard, but now it returned, spreading across my skin like cold fire. I released one hand from the reins to touch the dagger in my belt. My brother Henry had made it for me at our father's forge.

The sun dipped below the horizon just as I arrived at the caves. In the gloom, the entrance looked like a jagged black mouth in the hillside. My legs were weary from gripping the horse's heaving flanks, but I knew I couldn't fail the King.

I dismounted and drew out a torch from my saddlebag. With my tinderbox and flint, I lit a flame and held the blazing torch in front of me. The horse whickered, his nostrils flaring. From his wide eyes, I saw that he too sensed danger ahead.

"I go alone from here, friend," I whispered.

I took a deep breath and, with cautious steps, I entered the darkness. The torch threw a flickering orange glow onto the walls, making shadows like writhing snakes dance on the slick, moss-covered rock.

I felt a crunch and squelch beneath my feet. I lowered the torch. Hundreds of insects crawled and slithered over the ground. My heart thudded louder than a drum, but I pressed on.

As the tunnel dipped, the stagnant air wrapped around me like an icy embrace. I realised I could no longer see the entrance behind me. I reached a fork, so I followed the left-hand passage.

The torch sputtered and spat sparks, but thankfully it didn't go out.

I swallowed thickly, suddenly sure that I wasn't alone down here. Someone – or something – waited in the blackness.

With my free hand, I drew the dagger…

The scuttle of a rockfall made me turn around, and the flames licked across the wall, picking out a figure standing behind me with his hands tucked into his robe. My breath lodged in my throat.

"You!" I said. The wizard's apprentice smiled.

"Greetings, Taladon," he said.

"What are you doing here, Malvel?" I asked, sliding my dagger into its sheath. "Did Aduro send you to accompany me?"

"Something like that," he hissed.

My torch picked out the cruel glitter in his eyes. In a flash he drew his hands from his robe and I saw an orb of blue flame hovering between them. He flung out his arms and the fireball shot towards me. I ducked, stumbled, and lost my torch. It fizzled out on the wet ground.

"What do you want?" I asked, scrambling in the darkness behind a boulder. I couldn't believe what I was seeing!

"I want that shield," he replied. "Now come out and fight, *champion*!"

To be continued…

DIVE INTO THE BLACK OCEAN!

All you need to create Gorgonia's ocean depths is an empty shoebox and a monstrous imagination! Give your friends a shock by putting Narga into the scene...

YOU WILL NEED:

SHOEBOX
NEWSPAPERS
PENCIL
POSTER PAINTS
PAINTBRUSH
WHITE CARD
COLOURED PENS
SCISSORS
GLUE
SAND
PEBBLES
STICKY TAPE
PLUS
EXTRA ART
MATERIALS TO
DECORATE

1 Take the lid off your shoebox and set it to one side. Set the empty box on some old newspaper, then draw a faint backdrop to your scene on the inside.

2 Use paints to bring the backdrop to life. Don't forget to cover the entire back, sides, top and bottom of the box.

Think about drawing in dark swirling water, sharp rocks and strange sea plants. You might want to sketch some ideas first!

3 While the paint is drying, find a blank sheet of card and draw a picture of Narga. Make sure that the Beast is small enough to fit inside your scene.

4 Colour Narga in, then cut him out. Take care not to snip off any of his six heads! Now fold a 1cm crease along the bottom of the Beast.

5 Spread glue along the crease and stick Narga to the base of the shoebox.

6 Colour and cut out any other objects or characters you'd like to feature in your scene. Why not add in a shipwreck, or use a piece of cotton to suspend Tom from the top of the box, as if he is diving into the water?

WHY NOT ADD...?
BUBBLES MADE FROM MILK BOTTLE TOPS

SLIPPERY RIBBON EELS

SPIKY PIPE-CLEANER CORAL

7 Place some pebbles along the bottom of the box, or glue in a layer of sand. Add any other decorations to make the ocean seem even more scary, taping or sticking them in place.

8 When your Black Ocean is ready, ask an adult to help you cut a spyhole out of the centre of the lid. Tape the lid back on the box, then take a peek into the ocean's murky depths!

ELENNA

Elenna is Tom's best friend and has been with him on all of his Quests. She is armed with her trusty bow and arrows, and also her wits – Elenna's quick-thinking has often got Tom out of danger.

UNCLE LEO

When Elenna was a baby, a fire swept through the village where she lived. Her house was burnt to the ground and both her mother and father died. But Elenna's Uncle Leo tied a damp cloth around his face and burst through the blaze, grabbing baby Elenna and carrying her to safety.

Uncle Leo is a fisherman from southwest Avantia. He brought Elenna up, teaching her how to fish and sail a boat. Uncle Leo misses her when she's away on Beast Quests, but he knows that Elenna's tough enough to hold her own against any Beast.

SILVER

One day, when she was hunting in the woods, Elenna's foot caught in a tree root and she fell, twisting her ankle. A grey wolf padded towards her.

Elenna felt an immediate bond with him, and the wolf let her sit on his back while he carried her out of the woods.

This wolf was Silver. He became Elenna's loyal companion, and his bravery and speed would prove to be an enormous help on the Beast Quests.

SKILLS

Elenna never goes anywhere without her bow and arrow. Silver dug up her bow when they were hunting near the Winding River, and Elenna thinks it must have been used in an ancient battle before being buried. She makes most of her arrows herself, and long hours of practice mean that she rarely misses her target.

Elenna's mother was a healer, and the only thing that survived the terrible fire was her medicine book. With the book and tips from her uncle, Elenna taught herself how to use herbs and plants to heal cuts, wounds and infections.

Elenna's Brain-teaser

Tom doesn't just rely on Elenna's skill with a bow to help him – he needs her brains, too. Are you as sharp-witted as Elenna? See if you can answer her clues to fill in the grid below. When you've completed it, rearrange the letters in the green squares to reveal Elenna's friend.

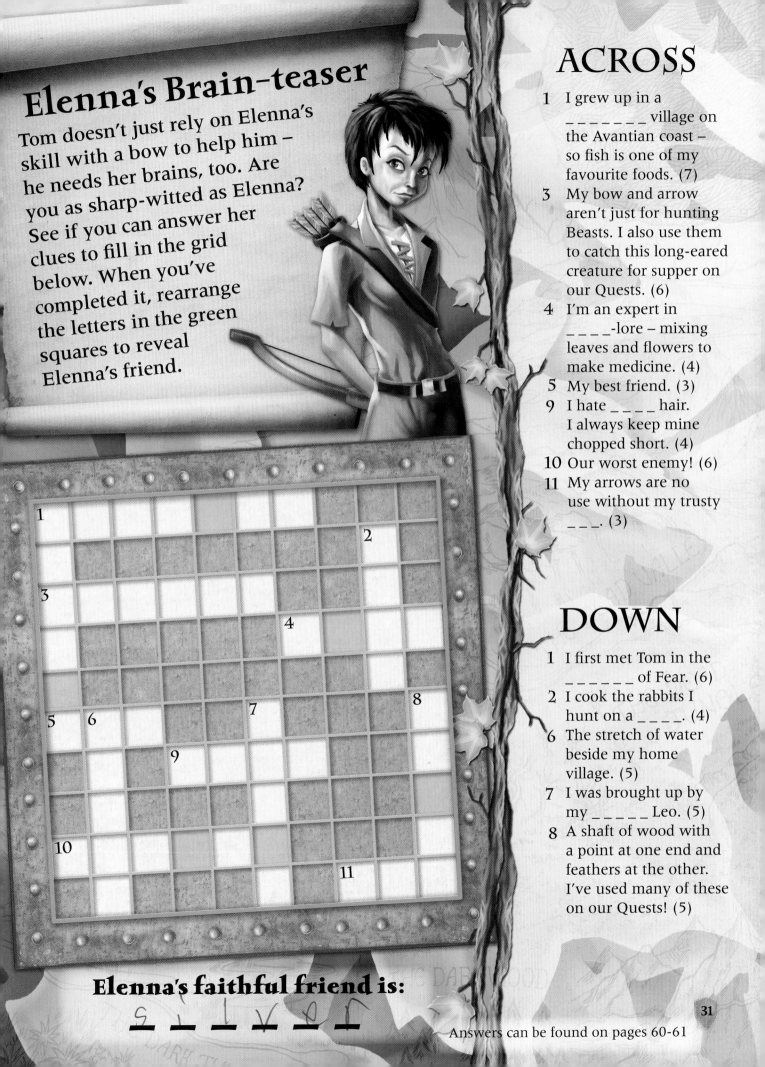

ACROSS

1 I grew up in a _ _ _ _ _ _ _ village on the Avantian coast – so fish is one of my favourite foods. (7)
3 My bow and arrow aren't just for hunting Beasts. I also use them to catch this long-eared creature for supper on our Quests. (6)
4 I'm an expert in _ _ _ _-lore – mixing leaves and flowers to make medicine. (4)
5 My best friend. (3)
9 I hate _ _ _ _ hair. I always keep mine chopped short. (4)
10 Our worst enemy! (6)
11 My arrows are no use without my trusty _ _ _. (3)

DOWN

1 I first met Tom in the _ _ _ _ _ _ of Fear. (6)
2 I cook the rabbits I hunt on a _ _ _ _. (4)
6 The stretch of water beside my home village. (5)
7 I was brought up by my _ _ _ _ _ Leo. (5)
8 A shaft of wood with a point at one end and feathers at the other. I've used many of these on our Quests! (5)

Elenna's faithful friend is:

S I L V E R

31

Answers can be found on pages 60-61

The Good Beasts of Avantia

When I first met Tom in the Forest of Fear, I believed that Beasts were only found in stories. But I was wrong – the creatures were real. We never cease to be amazed by the Beasts that we encounter, but our favourites are the Good Beasts of Avantia – they began as our enemies, but became loyal friends.

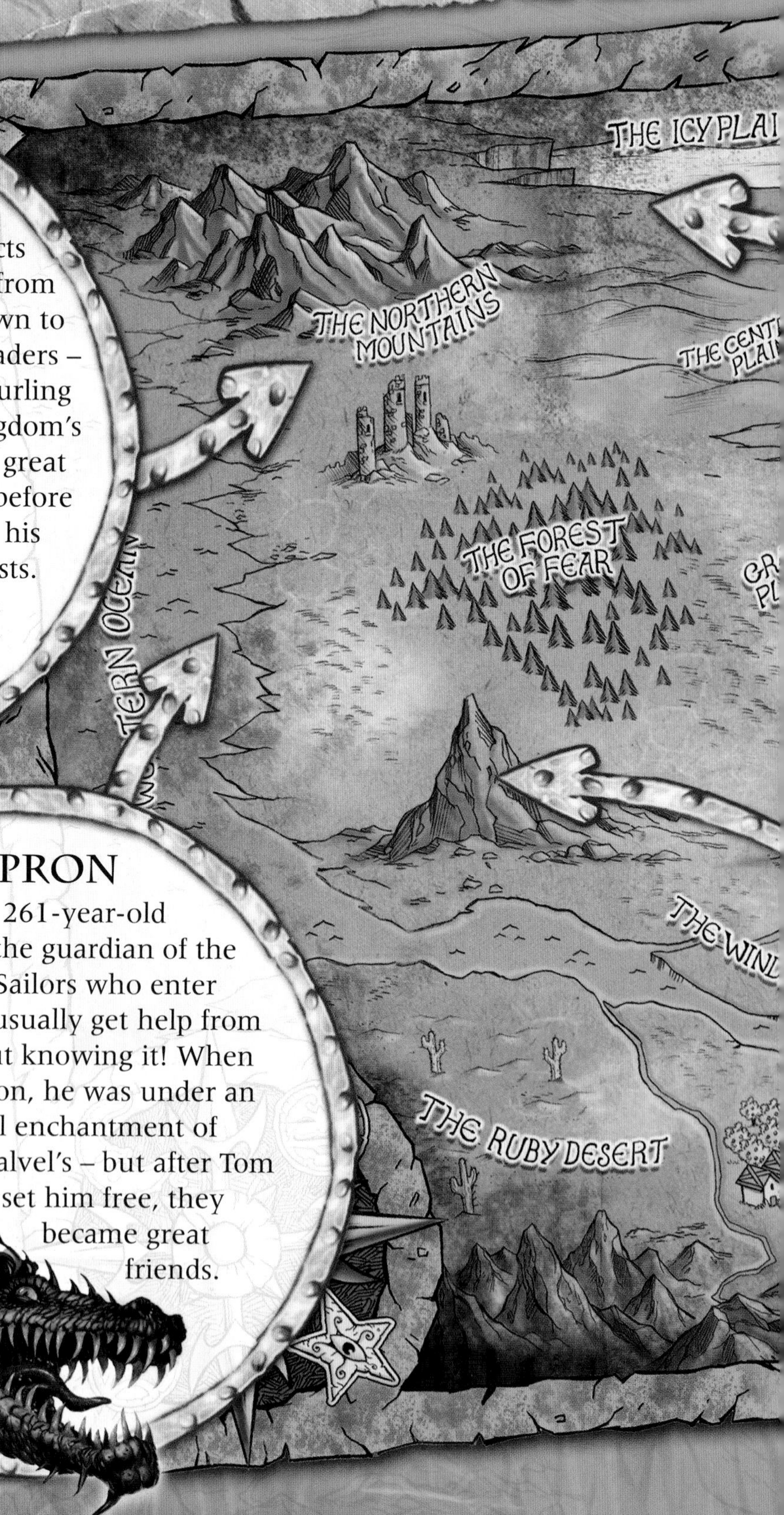

ARCTA

This giant, one-eyed Beast is 324 years old. He protects the mountain towns in the north from rock-falls. Arcta has also been known to protect the Avantian army from invaders – legend tells of him hurling boulders at the kingdom's enemies during a great war fought long before Tom began his Beast Quests.

SEPRON

Avantia's 261-year-old sea serpent is the guardian of the Western Ocean. Sailors who enter dangerous waters usually get help from this Beast – without knowing it! When Tom first met Sepron, he was under an evil enchantment of Malvel's – but after Tom set him free, they became great friends.

THE ICY PLAI

THE NORTHERN MOUNTAINS

THE CENT PLAI

THE FOREST OF FEAR

CR PL

TERN OCEAN

THE WINL

THE RUBY DESERT

NANOOK

Nanook is 335 years old, and is protector of Avantia's Icy Plains in the north – except during the warmest season, when she hibernates so that her heavy feet don't cause cracks in the ice. Malvel exploited this by placing an enchanted bell around her neck, preventing her from going to sleep – which made her very angry!

Hop, skip and
_ _ _ _ _

EPOS

Epos is 457 years old, which makes her the oldest of the Good Beasts. She has been a key figure in some of the most important tales in all of Avantian history. Long before Tom began his Quests, Epos was called Firepos. She also had a Chosen Rider, who would become the first Master of the Beasts. His name was Tanner.

MALVEL'S MAZE

STONEWIN VOLCANO

KING HUGO'S PALACE

THE CITY

ERRINEL

TAGUS

Brave Tagus is the second oldest of Avantia's Beasts, at 406 years old. He is the defender of the Central Plains. Tagus makes sure that no hyenas attack the cattle. He is faster than any horse, and stronger than any man – only the foolish get in the way of his deadly blade!

FERNO

The first Beast Tom and Elenna encountered, Ferno is also one of the most fearsome creatures in all the known worlds. He is 288 years old, and lives in the mountains and guards Avantia's Winding River. His fiery breath can turn trees to ash – not that he does that often. Ferno has been one of the noblest Beasts in the kingdom.

HE DARK

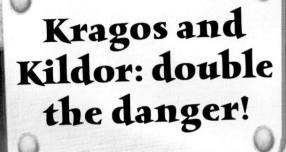

Kragos and Kildor: double the danger!

One of the deadliest enemies Tom has ever had to face is Kragos and Kildor the Two-Headed Demon! The Beasts share a man's torso covered in tough hide, muscular arms, and a ram's legs and sharp hooves. Two heads sprout from their neck – a ram's head with horns and a stag's head with antlers. But Kragos and Kildor's deadly power is that they can split into two! Kragos becomes a gentle-looking deer, while Kildor seems to be an ordinary sheep. But they use their harmless appearances to lure unsuspecting victims to their doom!

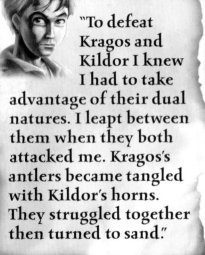

"To defeat Kragos and Kildor I knew I had to take advantage of their dual natures. I leapt between them when they both attacked me. Kragos's antlers became tangled with Kildor's horns. They struggled together then turned to sand."

"Kragos and Kildor are like the different sides of life. Day is always followed by night. Good is always challenged by evil. Kragos and Kildor will always use their double nature to attack."

34

KRAGOS AND KILDOR

Tom may have conquered Kragos and Kildor, but this isn't the end of the Two-Headed Demon... Every generation, Kragos and Kildor reform as a new Beast combining two new animals!

What do you think the new Kragos and Kildor will look like? The list of animals provided might give you some ideas.

Draw your Beast in the space below.

Bring Kragos and Kildor back to life!

Bear
Crocodile
Eagle
Lion
Rhino
Wolf

Vespick vs Kaymon

Mortaxe is at it again! This time, he has pitted two very different Beasts against each other in a deadly duel. This one is so close! Can you pick a winner?

If the battle on the ground gets difficult, Vespick can take to the air. She can launch aerial attacks that are tough to defend against.

Though armoured, Vespick is one of the smaller Beasts, and vulnerable to powerful strikes – especially from a Beast with the vicious jaws of Kaymon…

VESPICK

AGE	285
POWER	253
MAGIC LEVEL	173
FRIGHT FACTOR	96

Her sting is deadly. One strike, and no opponent can hope to survive.

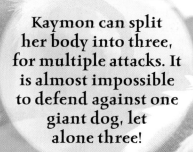

Kaymon can split her body into three, for multiple attacks. It is almost impossible to defend against one giant dog, let alone three!

KAYMON

AGE	296
POWER	165
MAGIC LEVEL	154
FRIGHT FACTOR	81

But is the Gorgon Hound too fast and too wild for her own good? If her quick attacks fail, her anger may cause her to make mistakes.

Kaymon's vicious teeth can rip almost anything to shreds. If she can catch her opponent in her jaws, the fight will be over.

AND THE WINNER IS...

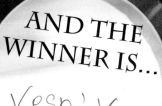

Vespick

TOM SAYS:
"I would not want to be caught in the middle of these two. If the Wasp Queen takes to the air, what tactic will the Gorgon Hound use? Too close to call!"

HEROES AND VILLAINS

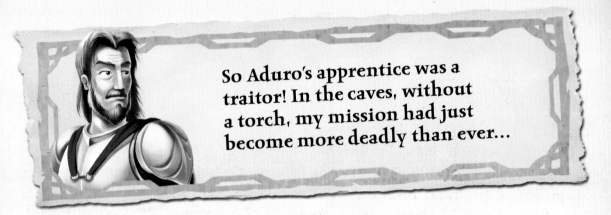

So Aduro's apprentice was a traitor! In the caves, without a torch, my mission had just become more deadly than ever...

From behind the boulder, I drew my dagger. But what use would it be against Malvel's spells and cunning? I saw the eerie blue glow of another fireball lighting up the cave wall. In moments he'd discover me, and then I wouldn't be so lucky.

I scrabbled on the ground, and found a loose rock half the size of my fist. I threw it at Malvel with all my strength.

THUMP!

"Ouch!" Malvel cried. I turned and ran deeper into the caves, my feet tripping on loose stones. I traced my fingers along the wall for guidance. Behind me Malvel roared, "Run all you want! I'll burn you to a cinder!"

There was a flash of blue light and a crunch of stone. Rocks and dust rained down on my head, but I rushed on blindly. I could hear Malvel's steps shuffling in pursuit.

"You'll pay for this!" I shouted. "When Aduro hears—"

"Aduro will never find out!" he called back. "Your body will be food for whatever creature dwells down here, and I will have the magic of the shield. King Theo will bow before me!"

His voice was filled with madness and lust for power. Ahead I saw that the path opened into a dimly lit cavern. Perhaps it was a way out… I quickened my steps, but my toe caught on something and I fell to my knees. Only now did I see that I was mistaken. The light came from a few shafts of moonlight piercing the cavern roof high above. I was trapped!

But it wasn't a rocky ledge that had tripped me. The faint moon-glow illuminated something lying on the path.

The shield!

As my fingers closed over it, Malvel appeared above me.

"So there you are!" he said, rolling another fireball between his palms.

It lit his face, making his features twisted and ugly. "It's time to put an end to your little quest, I think."

He hurled the fireball at my chest. I lifted the shield to defend myself and the flames crashed into the wood in a blinding flash. I felt as if a horse had kicked me, and I was aware of my body flying through the air. As I slammed into a rock wall, the shield fell from my grasp into a crack in the ground. In horror I watched it disappear into the darkness.

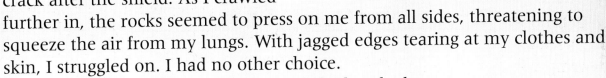

There was no time to think. Knowing that the next moment could be my last, I scrambled into the narrow crack after the shield. As I crawled further in, the rocks seemed to press on me from all sides, threatening to squeeze the air from my lungs. With jagged edges tearing at my clothes and skin, I struggled on. I had no other choice.

"You're like a ferret in a hole!" laughed Malvel.

I managed to twist my head and saw him at the other end, smiling cruelly at me.

"Well done, young hero!" he crowed. "You've managed to bury yourself alive!"

With a flash of blue, rocks fell over the end of the tunnel, blocking out the light completely. My escape route had become a grave. I thought of my home back in Errinel and the people I'd never see again. Worst of all, I thought of how I'd let down my King.

I lay there for what seemed a long time, a chill spreading through my bones, with only my shallow breathing to break the silence. *I'm going to die here*, I thought, gripping the shield. *No one will ever find me…*

A low rumble shook the rock walls, as if the cave itself had let out a huge roar. Then another crunch sent pebbles scattering. Suddenly, a huge section of rock lifted away and light flooded into the tunnel. I blinked and saw something I'll never forget.

Above me, its black wings silhouetted against the moonlight, hovered a dragon. It seemed to be made of the rock itself, cut from the very slopes. A tail waved magnificently beneath its massive body. It turned its head towards me, fire glowing in its jaws like the embers in my father's forge.

I gripped the shield and hoped that Aduro was right about its power.

To be continued…

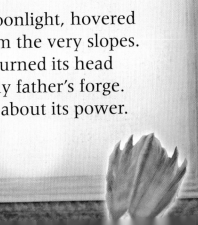

TOM'S QUEST MEMORIES...

It's not just Beasts that pose dangers for me. Sometimes, the land itself is just as dangerous – but that's what makes my adventures so exciting!

LIST YOUR TOP FIVE MOST EXCITING PLACES

1 ....

2 ....

3 ....

4 ....

5 ....

Tom's Top Five Most Exciting Places...

The Rainbow Jungle

When Elenna and I ventured to this jungle we found a wrecked Avantian ship in the middle of it. What was it doing there? A mystery we are yet to solve...

The Avantian Underworld

Two of my Quests have taken me to the Underworld, but I have a feeling there is much more down there still waiting to be explored!

The Golden Valley

In the dark goldmines of Kayonia lurks Fang the Bat Fiend – a Beast who can steal your sight!

Freeshor

The freezing cold North in Gwildor is home to Koldo the Arctic Warrior – and castles made out of ice.

The Stonewin Volcano

The home of Epos the Flame Bird – the hottest place I've ever been to, and one of the most dangerous.

When Tom won a yellow jewel in his Quest against Narga the Sea Monster, it gave him a perfect memory. How good is yours? Study the scene below for ten seconds. Then turn over and see if you can answer all the questions correctly.

NOW TEST YOUR MEMORY...

Read the questions below and use your amazing memory to recall the image on the previous page. The more questions you get right, the better your memory is!

1 Who is behind the cottage?

2 Do the footprints belong to a human or an animal?

3 Is Tom facing in or out of the picture?

4 How many horns does Bloodboar have?

5 Who is hatching from an egg?

6 What is in the sky?

Tom defends himself with a wooden
_ _ _ _ _ _

PETRA'S SPELL

Petra is magically holding Vedra and Krimon prisoner. Her magic can be broken with the right counter-spell. But the witch has jumbled up the words. Grab a pen and some paper and unscramble the letters below. Hurry – the young dragons are depending on you!

EST HTE RADNOGS ERFE

___ ___ _____ ____

43

Answers can be found on pages 60-61

THE WARRIOR'S SWORD

Wizard Aduro has asked Henry, Tom's uncle, to forge a new sword in his blacksmith's workshop. The sword is made from a magical metal that gives whoever uses it exceptional fighting skills. But Malvel has broken into the workshop and stolen it!

Can you get the sword back? Whoever finds it first will become a great warrior of Avantia!

START

HOW TO PLAY

You will need a dice, and a counter for each player. Place your counters on the start square, then decide who's going first. Roll the dice to see how many squares you can move. Good luck…

You find a trail of Malvel's footprints. Go forward four spaces.

You spot the sword glinting through the trees. Go forward four spaces.

Malvel attacks! Choose one player to be blasted back to the START.

You're charged by Bloodboar! Go back one space.

FINISH

You seize the sword from Malvel. You will become a great warrior of Avantia!

Malvel puts a freezing spell on you. Miss a turn.

Silver sniffs out Malvel's lair. Go forward two spaces.

Aduro appears in a vision. Go forward one space.

Balisk drags you into the Winding River. Go back four spaces.

You eat a supper of rabbit stew. Roll again.

Kronus picks you up and drops you back six spaces.

Malvel sends a swarm of bats to attack you. Miss a turn.

You fall into a trap woven from nettles and vines. Go back one space.

Torno grabs you in his jaws! Miss a turn.

Tom lends you his shield. Go forward three spaces.

Koron slashes you with his claws! Go back five spaces.

Hecton throws his trident at you. Miss a turn.

Elenna comes to your aid. Roll again.

45

PETRA'S POTION

The evil witch has mixed up a terrible potion in her cauldron. It will make Avantia's crops and trees die and even dry up the Winding River!

You must add a secret ingredient to her potion that will make it harmless. But can you work out what the ingredient is?

First you must find the words listed below inside the grid. Each word could be up, down, left, right or diagonal. Some words will share the same letters.

Aduro
Arax
Avantia
Balisk
Bloodboar
Bow
Claw
Elenna
Epos
Evil
Freya
Fur
Hecton
Hugo
Jaw
Kaymon
King
Koldo
Koron
Krabb
Kronus
Luna
Malvel
Murk
Nanook
Narga
Paw
Petra
Rashouk
Rion
Roar

H	W	A	P	E	T	R	A	O	B	D	O	O	L	B
E	L	E	N	N	A	V	A	N	T	I	A	W	D	R
C	L	A	W	O	L	F	R	E	Y	A	F	U	R	A
T	N	A	R	G	A	R	T	L	O	S	G	M	O	S
O	K	I	N	G	D	R	E	V	L	I	S	U	W	H
N	O	L	M	R	O	T	S	B	O	W	U	R	S	O
A	R	D	E	V	N	V	A	R	A	X	N	K	F	U
O	H	V	D	O	I	D	N	R	E	P	O	S	K	K
D	I	P	M	P	L	O	P	J	A	W	R	O	K	S
L	P	Y	E	E	P	B	A	L	I	S	K	T	O	M
O	A	R	I	Z	B	I	O	H	U	G	O	R	R	A
K	O	H	L	A	T	O	R	G	O	R	R	E	I	L
S	S	I	R	K	O	O	N	A	N	N	O	M	O	V
U	A	K	G	A	D	U	R	O	L	U	N	A	N	E
T	R	I	L	L	I	O	N	S	V	E	L	M	A	L

Rokk
Sanpao
Shield
Silver
Skor
Soltra
Storm
Sword
Tagus
Tail
Talad
Tom
Torg
Torn
Trem
Trilli
Tusk
Vedra
Velma
Vipero
Wolf
Zepha

Shade in each word as you find it. The unshaded letters will reveal the secret ingredient

Answers can be found on pages 60-61

PETRA'S PUZZLE

Oh no! Petra has put a memory spell on Tom. Now he can't remember what happened on many of his Quests – especially those that were long and dangerous. Can you answer the questions below and help Tom?

1 To which land did Tom have to take the baby dragons, Vedra and Krimon, to keep them safe?

2 Nawdren the Black Phoenix stole the body of which Beast?

3 Which winged mammal does Arax the Soul Stealer look like?

4 One of Kragos and Kildor's heads is a _____ with curled horns and the other is a _____ with jagged antlers.

5 What is Creta the Winged Terror's body made from?

6 Which Beast, who looks like a human skeleton, rose from the grave?

7 Ravira, Ruler of the Underworld, has leashes hooked through the palms of her hands. What creatures are attached to the ends of the leashes?

8 Which precious item did Kragos and Kildor steal?

Answers can be found on pages 60-61

Soltra's Spaghetti and Eyeballs

Just one gaze from the Stone Charmer's single eye turns her victims into solid stone! This spine-chilling spaghetti recipe is teeming with eye-shaped meatballs that stare up from the plate.

1 Ask an adult to preheat the oven to 190°C/375°F/Gas Mark 5.

2 Pour the olive oil into a deep-sided pan, then heat it gently on the hob. Finely chop the onion and garlic, then tip it into the pan.

Soltra's beastly meal will feed four hungry Quest seekers. To terrorize your dinner table tonight, you will need:

1 TABLESPOON OLIVE OIL

1 CLOVE GARLIC

1 ONION

2X400G CANS OF CHOPPED TOMATOES WITH HERBS

1 TABLESPOON OF TOMATO PUREE

SALT AND PEPPER

4 SLICES OF WHITE BREAD

750G LEAN MINCED BEEF

1 TABLESPOON OF TOMATO KETCHUP

1 MEDIUM EGG

1 TEASPOON DRIED BASIL

1 JAR OF GREEN OLIVES STUFFED WITH PIMENTO

250G DRIED SPAGHETTI

3 Once the onion and garlic have started to soften, pour the canned tomatoes in. Stir in the tomato puree, then add a touch of salt and pepper. Now that you've made your pasta sauce, turn down the heat and let it simmer.

Stay on your guard! Go back and check your pasta sauce every few minutes, stirring the tomatoes so they don't stick to the bottom of the pan.

While the sauce cooks, it's time to make your spooky Soltra meatballs! Tear the crusts off the bread, then ask an adult to help you turn them into crumbs using a blender. If you don't have one at home, you can buy ready-made breadcrumbs from most supermarkets.

4

5 Pour the breadcrumbs into a large mixing bowl, then add the mince, ketchup, egg and dried basil. Slowly stir the ingredients together.

6 Roll up your sleeves, then use your hands to mould 24 eyeball-shaped meatballs. Don't worry if they're not exactly the same size – some can be more bulgy than others!

7 Drain the olives from your jar, then press one into each of the meatballs. Make sure the bloodshot red pimento is facing outwards.

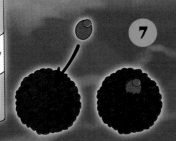

7

8 Find a baking dish and fill it with the meatballs. Give your pasta sauce a stir, then carefully spoon it over the top. Place the dish in the oven for 30 minutes.

8

9 When your meatballs are bubbling and ready to serve, turn the oven down to a low heat. Cook your spaghetti according to the packet instructions, then ladle it onto a serving plate.

10 Carefully take the baking dish out of the oven and lift the meatballs onto their bed of spaghetti. Spoon any extra sauce around the edge, then get ready to shock your supper guests!

HEROES AND VILLAINS

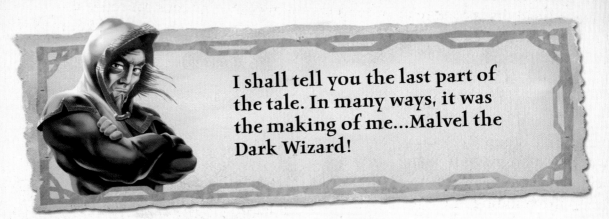

I shall tell you the last part of the tale. In many ways, it was the making of me...Malvel the Dark Wizard!

I left that foolish boy Taladon to a lonely death trapped in the dragon's cave, and rode through the night. I might not have had the shield, but no one else would get it either. Perhaps, one day, someone would find his skeleton clutching it, deep underground.

The portal glowed like a purple jewel in the sky. Long before I saw the battle, I heard the clash of swords and spears. *So, the Gorgonians have arrived!* I thought.

At the crest of a hill overlooking the battlefield, I surveyed the carnage. King Theo fought side by side with his son, leading his men from the front. I have to admit, young Hugo scrapped like a lion, driving at the enemy without thought for his own safety. But the Avantian band of fifty men was too small. Pitched against them were hundreds of Gorgonians pouring from the portal, bellowing war-cries. Aduro moved through the battlefield, swinging his staff and sending out bolts of green light, felling the enemy. But from my vantage point, I could see he too would soon be overcome.

"Help me, Malvel!" he shouted at me.

I didn't hurry. What was the point in risking my own skin for a lost cause?

One of the Gorgonians managed to knock Aduro's staff away, and another barged him with his shield. My old master collapsed to the ground. He managed to crawl away through the forest of legs. He reached my side and used my robes to haul himself to his feet.

"Taladon?" he asked.

I shook my head, and even managed to bring a film of tears to my eyes. "Dead by the time I got there, Master," I replied.

A shudder passed through Aduro and he lowered his face. "It's my fault. I should never have sent one so inexperienced." He surveyed the hopeless battle. "I'm getting old, Malvel. Perhaps it's time for a younger wizard to take over the kingdom…"

"Well, Master, if you insist…" My time had come!

Heavy metal object that stops a ship from moving

_ _ _ _ _ _

A sound like thunder split the air, louder than the battle below. The fighting ceased as men turned to look into the sky. Through the clouds burst a black head, its jaws spread wide to reveal dagger-like teeth, its red eyes burning. Scaled wings, barbed with hooks, heaved through the air. I felt my knees go weak.

"Ferno!" Aduro gasped.

But it was the boy perched on the Beast's back who chilled my blood. Taladon, his hair streaming and with the shield on his arm, waved down. As Ferno swooped over the plain, I saw fire building in his jaws. The Gorgonians screamed with terror, dropping their weapons, and running past us towards the portal.

Aduro fixed his eyes upon me, and suddenly looked more powerful than ever. "You lied to me, Malvel!" he said.

I retreated away from him. "You've held me back for too long," I said.

"I trusted you!" he roared. "And you betrayed me."

As Prince Hugo and his soldiers chased the last of the Gorgonians through the portal, King Theo pointed at me. "Take that traitor into custody!" he boomed.

I grinned. "You'll never catch me!" With a flick of my wrist, I shot a blue bolt at the King. He was too quick, and raised his sword, deflecting the magic. It rebounded into Kerlo's face.

"My eye!" he screamed falling to the ground and clutching his head.

I didn't wait to see how he fared. Seizing my opportunity, I ran for the portal. If Avantia was my enemy, then Gorgonia would be be my home. At its edge, I looked back to see Taladon soaring low on that wretched dragon. He pointed at me.

"One day we'll meet again!" he shouted.

I grinned as I stepped into the portal. "We will indeed!" I promised.

"Ferno was the first of the Beasts Taladon met, but more would follow. My father proved himself the saviour of Avantia that day, and Malvel became his sworn enemy. I'll never rest until he's defeated."

Arax vs Koldo

Arax's long barbed whip is one of the most frightening weapons I have ever faced on my Beast Quests – it once robbed the Good Wizard Aduro of his very soul!

ARAX

AGE	271
POWER	242
MAGIC LEVEL	187
FRIGHT FACTOR	92

Arax may be agile, but he is much smaller than Koldo. If he is struck by the Arctic Warrior, will he be able to recover?

The Soul Stealer can use his vicious clawed feet to kick or grab his opponents. With his bat-wings giving him a height advantage, defeating Arax is almost impossible.

TOM SAYS:
"This is another battle that is too close to call. Can Koldo catch Arax before his body melts? Can Arax keep his distance long enough for Koldo to tire, shrink and weaken? Who would YOUR money be on?"

Mortaxe has summoned two of the most dangerous Beasts of all to his Arena – Arax and Koldo. There can only be one winner...

Imagine being hit by a block of ice shaped like the biggest fist you've ever seen. It hurts!

KOLDO

AGE	335
POWER	183
MAGIC LEVEL	166
FRIGHT FACTOR	84

Koldo's ferocious ice club is a fearsome weapon that he wields with deadly accuracy.

AND THE WINNER IS...

Arax

As strong as he is, Koldo will need to defeat Arax quickly – the longer the fight goes on, the more his icy body will melt and shrink. If that happens, Arax might be able to pick him off.

TRAPPED!

Tom and Elenna are battling Sanpao and his pirate crew. But they've become lost inside the network of portals guarded by the Tree of Being! Can you help them find their way back to Avantia? Remember to avoid attacks from the pirates along the way...

Answers can be found on pages 60-61

Who is the Real Aduro?

The Evil Witch Petra has conjured a false Aduro! Look closely at these two pictures of Avantia's Good Wizard. The false Aduro has a spear instead of a staff, but can you spot the other five differences?

55

Answers can be found on pages 60-61

Can you choose the right token to defeat each Beast? Look out for the clues in the text below…

First to attack is KORON, JAWS OF DEATH. He pounds towards you, his feet kicking up clouds of sand that make it difficult for you to see him clearly. Suddenly, he's right in front of you! You need to lash out with one of your tokens, like a lion or a tiger would…

TOKEN: _Claw_

BALISK THE WATER SNAKE leaps out of the water, his body splitting in two. You must throw one of your tokens between his two bodies to stop them from reforming. Which do you choose?

TOKEN: _____

HECTON THE BODY-SNATCHER hurls his net at you. You fall to the ground, struggling under its folds. Hecton cackles, baring his teeth. They look sharp enough to bite through the net… Of course! You can use one of the tokens to cut through it.

TOKEN: _____

You can tie knots with this; rhymes with 'lope'

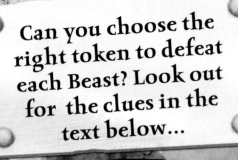

_ _ _ _

My friend, you are surrounded by Sanpao's Beasts! But don't worry. Remember the six tokens hidden among the pages of this book? You can now use them to defend yourself. Don't worry if you haven't found all the tokens yet. There's time to go back and search before the first Beast attacks...

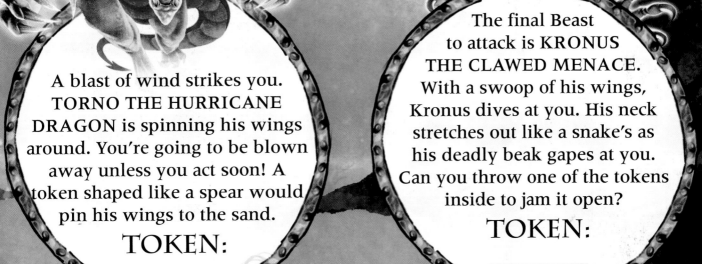

A blast of wind strikes you. TORNO THE HURRICANE DRAGON is spinning his wings around. You're going to be blown away unless you act soon! A token shaped like a spear would pin his wings to the sand.

TOKEN:

_____

The final Beast to attack is KRONUS THE CLAWED MENACE. With a swoop of his wings, Kronus dives at you. His neck stretches out like a snake's as his deadly beak gapes at you. Can you throw one of the tokens inside to jam it open?

TOKEN:

_____

BLOODBOAR THE BURIED DOOM lowers his head and charges at you. You dodge aside but he skids to a halt and turns, racing towards you once more. If you can roll something round at his feet, it will trip him...

TOKEN: _____

57

Answers can be found on pages 60-61

Showdown with Sanpao!

Have you found the six ships scattered throughout this annual and solved the six riddles? Each answer goes into one of the gaps in the story below. Can you fill them in correctly and defeat Sanpao?

You've caught up with Sanpao's ship on the coast of Avantia. Swimming silently through the water, you heave yourself over the side of the ship and roll onto the deck. The Pirate King's face twists with rage when he sees you.

    "Tom's interfering friend – I might have known!" Sanpau snarls. He lunges at you with his cutlass. You raise your _____ and deflect the blow.

    "You'll have to do better than that," you say.

    The Pirate King pushes a barrel. It rolls along the deck and you _____ onto it, then spring onto the rigging. You climb along, yanking down a huge blood-red _____ that hangs from the mast. It falls onto Sanpao, covering him.

    "Argh! Get this off me!" he yells.

    You leap onto the deck and grab a length of _____. Winding it round and round the struggling Pirate King, you tie the ends into a firm knot. Then you sprint across to the rope attached to the ship's _____. You pull on it, heaving the anchor up until it lands with a clang on the deck. The ship immediately begins to float upwards, out of the water.

    "So long, Sanpao!" you call.

    The Pirate King gives a furious growl. You climb onto the edge of the ship and jump down into the water. As you _____ to shore, you look up to see the ship flying across the sky, taking Sanpao away from Avantia.

Answers can be found on pages 60-61

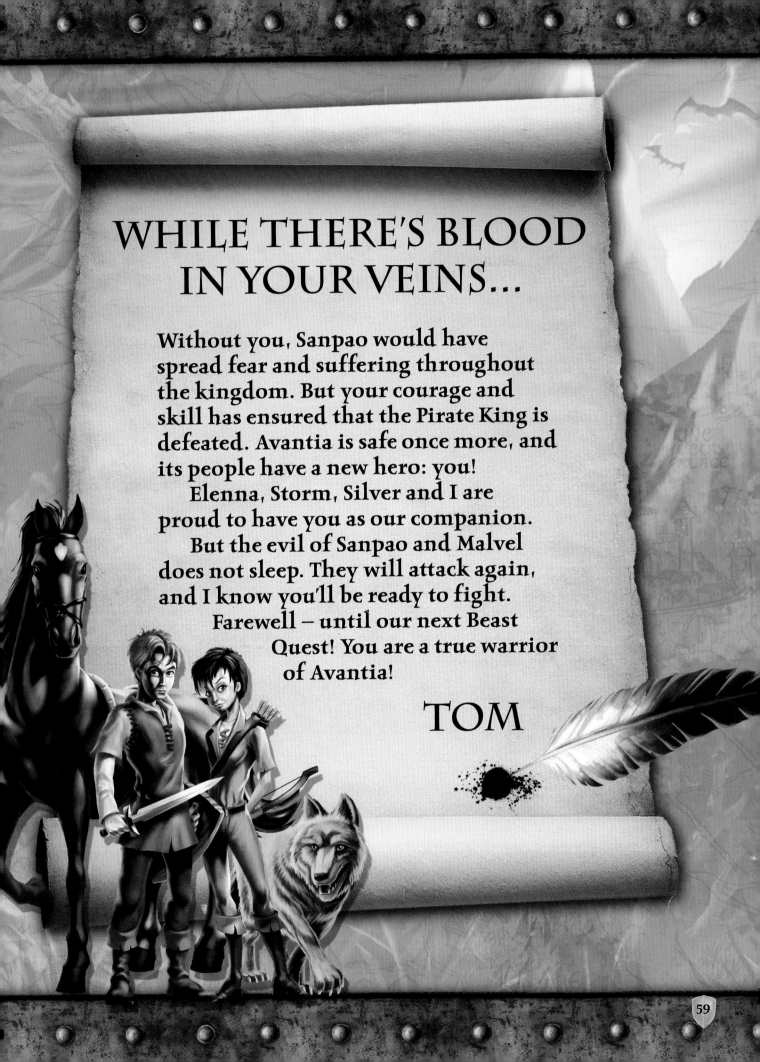

WHILE THERE'S BLOOD IN YOUR VEINS...

Without you, Sanpao would have spread fear and suffering throughout the kingdom. But your courage and skill has ensured that the Pirate King is defeated. Avantia is safe once more, and its people have a new hero: you!

Elenna, Storm, Silver and I are proud to have you as our companion.

But the evil of Sanpao and Malvel does not sleep. They will attack again, and I know you'll be ready to fight.

Farewell – until our next Beast Quest! You are a true warrior of Avantia!

TOM

ANSWERS

Page 16
Who am I?

The Beast is **Epos**

Page 17
Cross the Deadly Marshes

Page 25
Petra's Wicked Wizard Quiz

1   A (Velmal)
2   B (70)
3   C (The West)
4   B (Malvel)
5   C (Oradu)

Page 31
Elenna's Brain-teaser

Her faithful friend is **Silver**.

Page 41–42
What Can You See?

1 Silver
2 Human footprints
3 Tom is facing inwards
4 Eight horns (and two tusks)
5 Vedra
6 Fang the Bat Fiend

Page 43
Petra's Spell

The spell is SET THE DRAGONS FREE

Page 46
Petra's Potion

H	W	A	P	E	T	R	A	O	B	D	O	O	L	B
E	L	E	N	N	A	V	A	N	T	I	A	W	D	R
C	L	A	W	O	L	F	R	E	Y	A	F	U	R	A
T	N	A	R	G	A	R	T	L	O	S	G	M	O	S
O	K	I	N	G	D	R	E	V	L	I	S	U	W	H
N	O	L	M	R	O	T	S	B	O	W	U	R	S	O
A	R	D	E	V	N	V	A	R	A	X	N	K	F	U
O	H	V	D	O	I	D	N	R	E	P	O	S	K	K
D	I	P	M	P	L	O	P	J	A	W	R	O	K	S
L	P	Y	E	E	P	B	A	L	I	S	K	T	O	M
O	A	R	I	Z	B	I	O	H	U	G	O	R	R	A
K	O	H	L	A	T	O	R	G	O	R	R	E	I	L
S	S	I	R	K	O	O	N	A	N	N	O	M	O	V
U	A	K	G	A	D	U	R	O	L	U	N	A	N	E
T	R	I	L	L	I	O	N	S	V	E	L	M	A	L

The ingredient is Wolf Droppings.

Page 47
Can You Remember?

1 Rion
2 Spiros the Ghost Phoenix
3 A bat
4 Ram, stag
5 Insects
6 Mortaxe the Skeleton Warrior
7 Hounds
8 The Cup of Life

Page 54
Trapped!

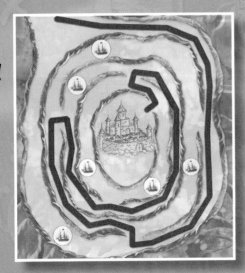

Page 55
Who is the Real Aduro?

Page 56–57
Beast Attack!

Koron = Claw
Balisk = Throwing star
Hecton = Fang
Torno = Trident
Bloodboar = Beast's Eye
Kronus = Scale

Page 58
Showdown with Sanpao!

Shield
Jump
Sail
Rope
Anchor
Swim.

Join the Tribe, Join the Quest

THE GOLDEN ARMOUR

978 1 84616 483 5   978 1 84616 482 8   978 1 84616 484 2

978 1 84616 988 5   978 1 84616 989 2   978 1 84616 990 8

THE DARK REALM

978 1 84616 997 7   978 1 84616 998 4   978 1 40830 000 8

978 1 84616 486 6   978 1 84616 485 9   978 1 84616 487 3

978 1 84616 991 5   978 1 84616 992 2   978 1 84616 993 9

978 1 40830 001 5   978 1 40830 002 2   978 1 40830 003 9

THE AMULET OF AVANTIA

978 1 40830 376 4   978 1 40830 377 1   978 1 40830 378 8

THE SHADE OF DEATH

978 1 40830 437 2   978 1 40830 438 9   978 1 40830 439 6

THE WORLD OF CHAOS

978 1 40830 725 0   978 1 40830 723 6   978 1 40830 726 7

978 1 40830 379 5   978 1 40830 381 8   978 1 40830 380 1

978 1 40830 440 2   978 1 40830 441 9   978 1 40830 442 6

978 1 40830 724 3   978 1 40830 727 4   978 1 40830 728 1

THE LOST WORLD

978-1-40830-729-8   978-1-40830-730-4   978-1-40830-731-1

THE PIRATE KING

978-1-40831-310-7   978-1-40831-311-4   978-1-40831-312-1

NEW SERIES! THE WARLOCK'S STAFF

978-1-40831-316-9   978-1-40831-317-6   978-1-40831-318-3

978-1-40830-732-8   978-1-40830-733-5   978-1-40830-734-2

978-1-40831-313-8   978-1-40831-314-5   978-1-40831-315-2

978-1-40831-319-0   978-1-40831-320-6   978-1-40831-321-3

COMING SOON! NEW BEAST QUEST SERIES: THE WARLOCK'S STAFF